Floyd

ATALANTA'S RACE
A Greek Myth

Retold by Shirley Climo

Illustrated by Alexander Koshkin

Clarion Books/*New York*

Clarion Books
a Houghton Mifflin Company imprint
215 Park Avenue South, New York, NY 10003
Text copyright © 1995 by Shirley Climo
Illustrations copyright © 1995 by Alexander Koshkin

The illustrations for this book were executed in watercolor, tempera, and gouache
on Waterman paper manufactured in Russia.
The text was set in 15/19-point Garamond.

Printed in the USA

Library of Congress Cataloging-in-Publication Data

Climo, Shirley.
 Atalanta's race : a Greek myth / retold by Shirley Climo; illustrated
by Alexander Koshkin.
  p. cm.
 Summary: Retells the myth of the Greek princess, rejected by her
father, raised by bears, won in marriage in a race by Melanion, and then
changed into a lioness by an angry Aphrodite.
 ISBN 0-395-67322-4
 1. Atalanta (Greek mythology)—Juvenile literature. [1. Atalanta
(Greek mythology) 2. Mythology, Greek.] I. Koshkin, Alexander, ill.   II.
Title.
BL820.A835C57   1995
398.21—dc20   94-26734
                    CIP
                    AC

BVG   10   9   8   7   6   5   4   3

For Nicole—
a runner, a winner!
—S.C.

For my friends
Gennady Spirin,
Valery Vasiliev,
Mikhail Fedorov
—A.K.

When the ancient world was young, and the gods kept a close watch on everything and everyone on earth, there lived a Greek king named Iasus. Iasus ruled the wild and mountainous kingdom of Arcadia. Here timid deer and hare shared wooded valleys with fierce bears and boars, while in the rocky heights above, eagles nested and sure-footed goats skipped among the boulders.

King Iasus lacked one thing in life. He and his queen had no children. There was no son to inherit Arcadia's throne.

Iasus prayed often to Zeus, greatest of the Greek gods, and to Rhea, the mother goddess: "I seek neither gold nor glory, but beg only for a son."

At last his plea was answered, and one wintry day a baby was born in the royal palace. But it was not a boy.

"A daughter!" roared King Iasus. "Why is Zeus punishing me by sending a girl?"

"Perhaps Rhea sent her as a reward," the queen replied. "I have named our child Atalanta."

"Call her what you wish, but she'll not stay in this house," vowed Iasus. "Guard!"

At once a soldier appeared in the archway.

"Take this baby," the king commanded, "and cast her on the highest slope of Mount Cyllene."

"But Atalanta will surely die!" the queen cried out.

Iasus raised his hands, palms up, to the sky. "Whatever happens to her is the will of Zeus."

The guard did not dare to disobey the king. He carried the baby up the snowy mountainside and laid her in the mouth of a cave, away from the bite of the wind.

The cave was the den of a she-bear. She heard Atalanta's whimpers and, curious, shuffled around the baby, sniffing. Then the bear opened her enormous jaws, picked up Atalanta, and took her inside the cave. She nestled the baby girl between her own two baby cubs and licked all three to sleep with her soft warm tongue.

The ice of winter melted. Spring turned to summer, summer faded to fall, and a full circle of new seasons had passed before Ciron, a hunter, stumbled upon the bears' den. He was tracking the she-bear, hoping for a bearskin to warm his bones. As he fit an arrow to his bow, he heard a scurry of footsteps inside the dark cave. Ciron leaned forward, squinting, and saw something crouching in the shadows. Boldly, he reached in and drew it into the sunlight.

"A child!" the hunter exclaimed.

The little girl looked at him and laughed.

Ciron had heard tales of Atalanta's birth and of the way she had been abandoned. Like most people in Arcadia, he thought that some beast had devoured her. But now he wondered.

"If you are the princess Atalanta," Ciron said to the child, "then the gods must have chosen me to care for you."

Ciron took Atalanta home to his woodsman's hut. He raised her as his own, told her nothing of her royal birth, and taught her the ways of the hunter. While other children played at hoops and knucklebones, Atalanta studied the tracks of deer and wolves. While other girls learned how to string a loom and weave, Atalanta learned to string a bow. She was steady of hand and so nimble that she could slip the honey from a hive without disturbing the bees.

By the time Atalanta was fifteen, she could speed an arrow to its target almost as well as Artemis, the goddess of the hunt, and she could even outrun a stag. But the day came when Atalanta was no longer content to race with fleet-footed deer.

"Must I always look at the world from the top of a mountain?" she asked.

"You are safe here," said Ciron.

"Why should I fear?" Atalanta stamped her foot. "I can take care of myself!"

"Only with the help of the gods," Ciron insisted, "for they see that each of us gets what he deserves."

"Then someday I shall wear a winner's crown of laurel," declared Atalanta, "for that's what *I* deserve!"

Soon after, Atalanta left, taking only her bow and arrows. She went first to Athens, then journeyed to Sparta and Corinth and Olympia. Although Atalanta could not compete in the Olympics—for females were excluded—she showed her skills in other contests. She won honors in the broad jump, in the discus throw, and even in wrestling. But it was in the footrace that Atalanta earned fame. In race after race, hers was the first hand to grasp the finish post.

Word of her triumphs spread throughout Greece. Reports even reached the ears of King Iasus.

"Bid this remarkable girl to come to court," he ordered.

So Atalanta returned to the royal house where she had been born, to the palace of King Iasus.

Iasus studied the tall maiden standing straight as a spear before him and asked, "Are you the one they call 'the pride of the woods of Arcadia'?"

"I call myself Atalanta of Arcadia," she replied.

"Atalanta?" The king paled. "How came you by that name?"

"I am told my first mother named me so. My second mother was a she-bear on Mount Cyllene."

"And your . . . father?" the king whispered.

"Ciron the hunter found me in the bear's den," said Atalanta. "He is my only father."

"It is time that you met another," said King Iasus.

Then the king spoke of things that Ciron had feared to mention. He told Atalanta about her birth and how she came to be cast on the mountain. "I was wrong," said Iasus. "Forgive me."

Atalanta stared coldly back at him. "And my mother?" she asked. "What of her?"

"The queen has long since died, and I am alone." The king hung his head. "I pray you will remain to keep me company."

Atalanta was silent, thinking. She could leave her father as he had once left her. But now King Iasus was bent with age, and the hair beneath his crown was as white as thistledown.

"I will stay," she decided.

Princess Atalanta wanted for nothing in the House of Arcadia. She carried her arrows in an ivory quiver, and her sword and shield were hammered from the strongest bronze. Two fine horses were added to the royal stable so that Ciron could join Atalanta in the hunt.

King Iasus watched Atalanta with pride and pleasure, but his happiness was not complete. He yearned for a grandson to sit on Arcadia's throne.

"You should marry," he told Atalanta. "Is there no one you love?"

"Love!" she said. "I do not believe in it."

"Take care!" cried Iasus in alarm. "What if Aphrodite, the goddess of love, should hear you?"

Atalanta shrugged. "What that goddess overhears is no concern of mine."

When months had passed, and Atalanta had turned away one suitor after another, Iasus grew impatient. "With love or without it, I order you to wed!"

Atalanta smiled sweetly at her father and asked, "May I choose my husband in my own way?"

"Indeed!" Iasus agreed. "Choose whom and how you will."

"Then he who can outrun me in a race will win my hand," she declared, "but he who loses will lose his head."

Atalanta was pleased with her scheme. What man would risk his life so foolishly?

Atalanta picked a grassy valley where a curved track was laid out for the competition. Broad steps were cut into the hillside for the judges and the spectators to sit and watch the race. When the preparations were complete, King Iasus sent out messengers with a proclamation:

Be it known that any man of any nation who can outdistance Princess Atalanta of Arcadia in a race shall win her in marriage. The penalty for defeat is death.

Soon the Arcadian court swarmed with Greeks and Cypriots, Sicilians, Egyptians, and Ethiopians. Among the athletes were Olympic winners, confident of outrunning a woman. Others, less famous, simply wanted to wed the beautiful princess.

The arrival of so many suitors dismayed Atalanta. Some were even too young to grow beards.

"Withdraw from the contest," she begged each one. "To do so is no dishonor."

A few listened. Those who did not lost their races and their lives.

Among the judges was a young Greek warrior named Melanion. He was hailed as a hero, and was an athlete in his own right. When Melanion first saw Atalanta, he thought she looked like any other mortal maiden. But when he saw the princess run, her hair streaming behind her like a cloud, beautiful as a goddess, he was determined to win her hand in marriage.

"No!" cried Atalanta when Melanion bid for the race. "A hero should not throw away his life."

"Give me the same chance you have given other men," Melanion insisted.

"If you must." Atalanta sighed. "Tomorrow, as soon as Apollo drives his sun chariot into the sky, we shall race."

17

Melanion slept badly that night. Strange images danced before him. Aphrodite, the goddess of love, appeared on a beam of moonlight and offered him three apples of purest gold. They were so bright they dimmed the stars above.

"With these apples you can win Atalanta's race," the goddess said, "and so teach that too-proud girl a lesson."

Melanion gazed at the golden apples. "How shall I use them?" he asked.

"That you must find out for yourself," Aphrodite answered, and vanished as suddenly as she had come.

The sun awakened Melanion. As he jumped from his couch, three gold apples tumbled to the floor. Melanion thrust them into his tunic and hurried to the track.

Atalanta already stood on her starting stone, digging her toes into the grooves. When Melanion smiled at her, Atalanta's face flushed a brighter pink than the morning sky.

"Withdraw, Melanion," she pleaded, "for my sake as well as yours."

"I come to run with you, not away from you," he protested.

The trumpet sounded a single note, and the race began.

Melanion ran with long, even strides, his feet thumping the hard-packed dirt like drumbeats. Atalanta skimmed over the ground as lightly as a dragonfly, not even raising a puff of dust. They finished the first length side by side.

Lifting his chin, Melanion charged ahead in the second length. Atalanta watched him with admiration, but she did not let him outdistance her for long. With quick, soundless steps, Atalanta flew past him. "Farewell, Melanion," she called.

Melanion panted at her heels, but with each breath he fell farther behind. Then he remembered Aphrodite's golden apples. Snatching one from his tunic, Melanion tossed it on the track.

The apple rolled to a stop in front of Atalanta.

"How beautiful!" she exclaimed. She slowed, bending to pick up the gleaming apple. Melanion dashed past her.

Atalanta began to run as if she were chasing the wind. Just as she drew even with Melanion, he cast another golden apple at her feet.

"For you, Atalanta!" he shouted.

This apple was bigger and brighter than the first. Atalanta could not resist such a treasure. She paused to scoop it up.

Even with a heavy apple in each hand, Atalanta easily caught up with Melanion. She saw him hold his side in pain. Once he stumbled and almost fell. For the first time, Atalanta was not happy to be winning.

In desperation, Melanion hurled the third apple. It rolled along the border of the track, glinting like a piece of sun in the green grass.

Atalanta ran on, chanting to herself, "Make haste! Make haste!"

But, soft in her ear, she heard different words. "Take the apple! Take the apple, Atalanta! Aphrodite picked it just for you."

Atalanta hesitated. Perhaps it was the wind whispering in her ear. But, perhaps . . . She bent down and scooped up the third gold apple.

Clutching all three apples, Atalanta began her sprint for the finish. Now she could hear the voices of the spectators. "A-ta-lan-ta! A-ta-lan-ta!"

Then she heard them chant, "Melanion! Melanion! Melanion!"

Atalanta looked back. Melanion was so close that she could feel his breath. Just ahead was the winning post. Atalanta leaped toward it. But Melanion's hand stretched over her shoulder and touched the post first.

Melanion had won the race!

Atalanta gasped. Then she looked at Melanion and smiled. Losing the race was a small price to pay for finding love.

Atalanta married Melanion. When their son, Parthenopaeus, was born a few years later, King Iasus was happiest of all.

Atalanta and Melanion lived a carefree life, riding together in the

hunt and competing in many sports. They were too busy to honor the gods. They never offered thanks to Aphrodite for her gift of the golden apples.

Angry, Aphrodite complained to the mother goddess, Rhea. "Those two care only about the hunt and games and races."

"If that is all they desire, then that is all they shall have," Rhea decreed. "Let them race and hunt forevermore."

She clapped her hands, and Atalanta turned into a lioness. Rhea clapped again, and Melanion changed into a lion.

And that, so ancient poets said, was how Atalanta's story ended—for that was the will of the gods.

AUTHOR'S NOTE

Atalanta's Race is an ancient Greek myth. It was told for many hundreds of years before the Roman poet Ovid recorded it in the first century. Sometimes this tale was set in Boetia instead of Arcadia. Sometimes Atalanta's father was named Schoenius and Melanion was called Hippomenes. But Atalanta was always the same. She may have been a real person, for this remarkable girl appears in other Greek legends as well.

Many statues and pictures from Greece of long ago show Atalanta and Melanion as lions guarding Rhea's throne or pulling her chariot. One old account described the lioness and lion as running freely though the woodlands in a never-ending race. Perhaps that is a happy ending for Atalanta and Melanion after all.

The ancient Greeks believed that strength and talent were gifts granted by the gods, so they held competitions as special offerings to the gods. The Olympic games were founded more than 3500 years ago to honor Zeus. A flame burned on his altar throughout the events. That is why a lighted torch is the symbol of today's Olympics.

Early **Olympic** competitions **had only** one **race. Known** as a stade, it was a sprint the length of the field, about 200 meters. Our word stadium comes from that measure. Later, other contests were added, including some in music and the arts. Atalanta's famous race was about the length of a present-day 1500-meter run.

Since 1900, track and other Olympic events have been open to women athletes. Atalanta would be pleased.

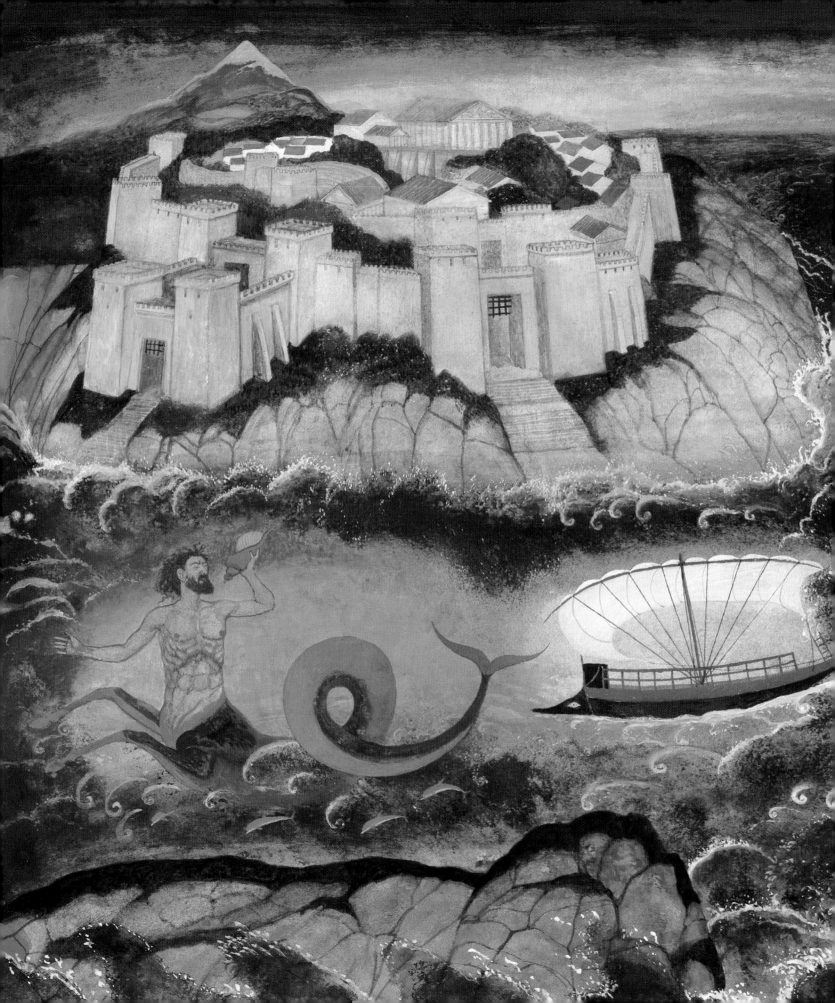